PEARLY GATES

Pearly Gates

PARABLES FROM
THE FINAL THRESHOLD

Sarah Hinlicky Wilson

THORNBUSH PRESS

Thornbush Press | www.thornbushpress.com

Cover design and artwork by Andy Bridge
Book Layout © 2017 BookDesignTemplates.com

Pearly Gates: Parables from the Final Threshold / Sarah Hinlicky Wilson.
-- 1st paperback ed.
ISBN 978-1-7352300-2-3

Contents

*And the twelve gates were twelve pearls,
each of the gates made of a single pearl...*

—Revelation 21:21a

This Is
Your Body

THERE ONCE WAS A mean-spirited old lady who liked no one and was liked by no one.

The only joy she found in this life was in her contrary ways. She cooed during the renunciation of the devil at her baptism but screamed with all her breath when the water splashed over her furrowed red forehead.

On the day of her confirmation she refused to recite the Creed. The flummoxed pastor laid his hands on her anyway for the sake of the public. Later he warned her: "The ceremony did not take."

In school she deliberately gave the wrong answer and argued when the teacher tried to correct her. In time, no teacher would call on her even if hers was the only hand in the air. This gave the girl deepest satisfaction.

When she left school, her beauty caught the eye of a handsome and mild-mannered fellow. He took her contrary ways to be maidenly wiles and, thus deceived, married her, but she did not desist upon becoming a matron. Her husband became a very successful businessman since he was motivated to be at work as often as possible, and she gave him a measure of peace as long as she had full run of his money.

Only one child came of the marriage, a son who learned to keep his thoughts to himself and give his mother what she wanted. When he grew up, he went to live far, far away.

So the years passed, and the young woman grew to be an old woman with no friends, a defeated husband, and an estranged son. To strangers at the grocery store and in the library she spoke bitterly of the cruelties of this life and the impossibility of God in the face of all the evidence.

Her husband died; she lived alone; and the years crept past.

At last the old lady felt herself approaching death. She summoned her son, who came guiltily across the country to tend to her in her dying hour. She lay on the bed, her breathing labored, and instructed him to fetch a pastor to bring her the Lord's Supper.

The son was not a little astonished by this, for, as his mother had so often told him, she hadn't darkened the door of a church since the day of her invalid confirmation.

But the woman was insistent, so her son went in search of a pastor.

Two days passed before the son could bring to his mother a willing pastor with a free moment. In that time the old lady worsened considerably. She was no longer conscious, no longer eating or drinking, only drawing loud but shallow breaths, one at a time. Her son expected each breath would be her last.

The pastor spent some time holding her hand and looking at her face. At last he said, "She cannot eat the bread or drink anything anymore. I'll just say a prayer to commend her to God."

But the son said, "Never in her life has she said one good thing about God or the church or anything connected with it. Even if she's lost her mind, I must see to it that she gets what she wants. She must have it."

The pastor shrugged and said, "I will put it in her mouth, just a piece of it."

So the pastor said the words and placed a small fragment of the bread saturated in wine inside the gaping mouth of the old woman. Not ten seconds after he did, her breathing stopped, and she died.

Then the woman found herself no longer on her bed at home, but standing at a gate guarded by an apostle.

The apostle said to her, "What do you want?"

The woman said, "I want to come in."

The apostle said, "Why should I let you in?"

The woman said, "I cannot tell you. I can tell only the Lord himself. Fetch him here and I will explain myself to him."

The apostle showed no surprise at the impertinence of the woman's request but retreated behind the gate. Some time later he returned, accompanied by the Lord in person.

"My friend tells me you wish to come in," said the Lord.

"I do," said the woman.

"He says you would like to tell me why I should let you in."

"I would," said the woman.

"Then tell me," said the Lord.

"I am a mean old woman," she said. "I have never loved anybody. I have never done a kind thing in my life. I scoffed at you and burdened all the people you sent to me."

The Lord nodded gravely.

"But if you do not let me in," said the woman, "you will never be complete."

The Lord looked at her. "How can this be?"

The woman opened her mouth and drew out the wine-soaked fragment of bread. "Here is a piece of your own body and blood," she said. "If you do not let me in, I will keep it for all eternity. Then whatever joys you have in there without me, you will always know a piece of you is missing."

The Lord lifted up his face and laughed. He turned to his apostle and said, "Behold, my friend, I have not found such faith as this in all the church!"

Then he turned to the woman and said, "I would not remain incomplete. Come in through the gate, leave your burdens behind you, and enter into the joy of the Lord."

And the woman did just that.

Suitcase

A MAN STOOD BEFORE the gates of the New Jerusalem. As he had expected, for he was well-read in the Scriptures, it glowed like jasper yet was clear as crystal, four-square, adorned with every kind of jewel. Each of the twelve gates was carved out of a single luminous pearl, and a street of transparent gold stretched out from each pearl, wending toward the throne of God.

"Never," said the man to himself, "have I wanted anything as much as I want to enter this beautiful city." And he was pleased at the intensity of his devotion.

He approached one of the gates. An apostle presented herself.

"Welcome," said the apostle.

"Thank you," said the man. "I am ready to be at rest."

"It awaits you," said the apostle. Yet she stood at the center of the gate, such that the man could not pass.

"Excuse me," said the man politely. "I cannot get around you."

"You may enter," said the apostle, "but that cannot enter with you." She pointed.

The man was surprised. He looked down at his own hand, where the apostle was pointing, and discovered that he was holding a suitcase. "I don't remember this," he said. "I'm sure I didn't bring it with me when I died. I don't even know what's in it."

"In that suitcase," said the apostle, "are many things you have loved."

"God is love," said the man.

"They are the things you ought not to have loved," said the apostle, "and the things you loved more than the Most Lovable of all."

The man was silent. At once he knew what was in the suitcase. Indeed, he loved the things within it very much.

"The suitcase cannot enter. But you can," said the apostle.

The man turned away a little from the apostle. He regarded the suitcase for a long time. He did not want to leave it. He wanted still to love it.

"But they are part of me," he said at length.

"They cannot come in," said the apostle.

The man contemplated further. "I will not be complete without them," he said.

"You will be more complete when you have lost them," said the apostle.

The man stood for a long time outside the gate. He looked through to the golden city; he looked down to the suitcase.

At last it seemed to the man that the apostle's attention was distracted. All at once he dashed toward the gate. Faster than the apostle he leapt through the pearl frame and landed on the gold street on the other side.

But the suitcase was no longer in his hand.

With a cry of anguish he turned back and leaned out the gate. The suitcase lay outside the walls of the city. He reached toward it.

"It cannot enter," repeated the apostle.

The man pushed past the apostle, out of the gate and out of the city. He picked up his suitcase. He hugged it. He took a few steps away from the gate and sat down, leaning against the outer wall of the city, cradling the suitcase in his arms.

"I will never let you go again," he crooned.

Night Cloak

A WOMAN APPROACHED THE gates of heaven. She was dressed in a cloak. It covered her whole body, from the hood on her head to the hem that swept around her feet. It was the color of night and kept her well concealed.

Slowly and cautiously she walked all the way round the city. It took her a long time, for the city was very large. Everywhere the gates stood wide open; anyone could see in. This distressed her. She could see the people moving through the radiant light inside. She could not see sun or moon or stars, but from the center of the city something bright, brighter than the sun but not painful to the eyes, shone out, sending its beams everywhere. Even the shadows in the city glowed.

At last she came back to where she'd begun. Not wishing to remain outside any longer but fearing the light within, she approached an apostle standing by the gate. She kept her head bent down. She tried to think of what to say.

"Come in, sister," said the apostle in a kindly voice. "The door is open."

The woman wrapped the cloak tightly about her, took a deep breath, and prepared to step across the portal.

"Sister," said the apostle, holding up a gentle hand, "that cloak will be of no use to you within."

"I cannot give it up!" she cried.

"I do not ask you to give it up," he answered her. "You may take it in. But it will cease to be of use."

"I will still be glad to have it."

"You believe it will conceal you, but it will not. There is no night in this city. The cloak will turn to the colors of the day; nothing will be hidden under it."

At this the woman shrank back. She stepped as far from the gate as she dared.

"No harm will come to you," said the apostle in the same kindly tone. "No harm can come to you. It is all locked away forever."

"I do not fear harm," replied the woman. Still she would come no closer.

"Then what do you fear?"

For a long time she would not speak. At last she said, "I fear for the others who will see me."

"As no harm can come to you, no harm can come to them, either."

"But you have not seen me," protested the woman.

"I am not afraid. Nor are the others."

"You do not know me!" cried the woman in a piercing tone. "I tell you, I am terrible to see. For I am covered in scars. I have been wounded grievously and never healed. My eyes are rimmed with exhaustion and mistrust. My hair lies thin and lank on my head. In some places I bleed. The injuries in me carry the pain, and the memory of the pain, and they will not let it go, not even when I have pleaded with them to release and forget. I am ugly, ugly, ugly! The people within will look on me and know that harm has come into their city. They will hate me and send me out again. I can only stay if I am cloaked so that none will see what I have become!"

"In this city," said the apostle, in the gentlest tone yet, "all things are seen. Nothing can be cloaked or concealed."

"Then," said the woman in the tones of deepest despair, "I should stay out. For it is better to keep out the bearer of misery than to have the peace of many be poisoned."

"That is not the way we reason here." The apostle stepped away from the door. He approached the woman very slowly. "If you like," he said, "I can wrap you in my own cloak, and walk in with you, so that the people will see the apostle, not the sister who walks with him."

"Will you stay there with me?"

"You will not need or wish me to stay," he answered. "But come now."

She allowed the apostle to wrap part of his own cloak about her. It was the many colors of a sunrise. She winced when his hand touched hers, but then relaxed, for it did not hurt. He took a step forward. He waited till her step matched his. So they proceeded to the gate, and through it.

Within the city the woman cried out for joy and amazement at the colors of jade and jasper and carnelian and gold, the healing scents of the leaves on the trees and fresh-running water, the glories being sung in many tongues and by many choirs. She felt a heart's ease that she had not known in all the earthly life that she could remember. She simply stood and breathed; she did not know how long; perhaps for centuries.

At last the apostle said, "You do not need my cloak."

"But I still have my own!"

"You do. But you do not need it, either." He stepped away, and his cloak fell away from her shoulders. Her night cloak was struck by the light from the center of the city. Its fibers trembled, grew, shrank, and all at once fell away like tiny, shiny feathers drifting to the ground. The woman was uncovered.

She looked down at her body.

She was whole and beautiful.

And all who gazed on her saw her beauty and loved her, and she no longer feared their gaze.

Another Lord

THERE WAS A MAN who worshiped and loved a lord who was not the Lord. He devoted all of his life to this lord's service, wrote hymns and tracts and books, taught and explained, and brought others to faith in this lord. He was a kind man and wise about his own soul and eager, when he died, to meet the one whom he had served and adored so long.

Then he found himself before the gates of heaven faced with the Lord who was not his lord.

"Who are you?" he said.

"I am the Lord," said the Lord.

"But is my lord not the Lord?"

"He is not."

"And where is he?"

"He is here. He now recognizes me as Lord, though he did not know me before."

At this the man grieved, for he did not know the Lord, and did not love him, and longed for his own lord.

"Can I not see my lord?" he asked.

"You will see him, when you recognize the same Lord that he does."

The man withdrew. His sorrow felt as deep as eternity. He sat down and grieved. It was a long grief.

At last after some unaccountable time the man arose and returned to the gate. The Lord waited for him still.

"Would you come in?" the Lord asked him.

"I would," said the man, "but I cannot yet. For I do not know you and I do not love you. But I do love my lord, and if he calls you his Lord, then I must do the same. So teach me how to love you that I may both be with him and recognize you."

The Lord said, "Wait at the gate, then, and greet those whom you knew and taught in the life before. They will grieve also like you, but not as deeply as you have grieved. Teach them that I am the Lord so that they may know my ways. Then you will come to love me."

These were sore words for the man, for he had hoped the new love would come easily. But he still longed for his old lord and knew he could not be made right with him until he was made right with the true Lord.

So they came, one by one, sometimes in twos, those he had known before. He met them at the gate and taught them of the new Lord. They were surprised, and sometimes sad, and some had to withdraw to grieve, but never so long as had the man himself. They asked questions he could not answer, so he returned to the Lord to ask for the answer, and then he brought the answer back to them. This he did dutifully but without joy, while many passed through the gates and left him outside.

At last there came an end to those he had known and taught. He found in his soul that he trusted the Lord but still did not love him.

"Shall I enter now?" he asked of the Lord. "For those I have taught have all come in."

"Do you love me?" asked the Lord.

"I do not," said the man.

"There are now coming those," said the Lord, "whom you did not meet in the flesh, but who have read your words, and so have come to a faith in your lord. These also you may teach."

So the man remained outside the gate and waited for those who had read his words. As they came he taught them, and they came to trust and love the Lord.

But soon the man realized that there would be no end of those who read his words, and if he should wait till the end, he should never enter the gates. Yet he found his heart still cold toward the Lord.

At last there came one who had read the man's words and believed in the other lord. He did not greet the news of the true Lord with joy, or even sadness: he greeted it with anger.

"I will have none of this new Lord," the second man said to the first one.

"He is not a new Lord, but the oldest Lord of all," said the first.

"He is a scandal and a charlatan. Who can believe what is said of him?"

"It is true. I have seen the wounds myself."

"Then it is true. But he will not win me with his wounds. He is not what I wanted in the life before and he is not what I want now."

"You cannot be right with our lord until you are right with this Lord."

"Then I will not have either. I will have no lord."

"You will always have a lord. If you will not have the Lord, or our lord, you will have only yourself as lord."

"Then I shall be a lord. And you shall be one too! Come away with me and we shall be lords together."

"But without the Lord I can never see the lord we once had."

"He is a scoundrel and a charlatan, too, who taught us amiss."

"He did not know."

"It is no excuse. There is no need for other lords now. You know what is true and can choose in knowledge instead of fumbling in faith. Come with me!"

The first man then grieved more deeply than ever, for he felt in his heart the bitterness of a life of false faith. And he saw for the first time the possibility of a choice made in full knowledge. The temptation was very great.

But greater still was his love for his old lord.

And when he knew that his love for his old lord was greater than the desire to be his own lord, he also knew that he had begun to love the true Lord, who loved and forgave the one who had taught and led others in a false faith.

"Do not be your own lord," he said to the second man, "but come with me into the joy of this true Lord."

The second man would not be persuaded. The first man delayed his entry into the gates in hopes of changing the heart of the second, but it was no use. At last the second man walked away and disappeared from the first man's sight.

This was the greatest grief of all.

At last when he saw there was nothing he could do, the man turned and approached the gates.

The Lord asked him, "Do you love me?"

The man said, "Yes, Lord, I love you."

And he entered in and was united with his old lord, and the two of them together with their new Lord, and all of heaven rejoiced.

Noli Me Tangere

AT THE GATES, A woman said to the Lord, "I think I would like to come in. It is cold and dry out here, and it looks warm and green in there."

"But sister," said the Lord, "you don't believe in me."

"Of course I do!" protested the woman. "I see you standing right there in front of me."

"Blessed are those who see and yet believe," he answered her. "I will show you your unbelief. Reach out and touch my side."

The woman hesitated.

"You see here the wound," he said, pointing to his side. "Put your fingers in it. Touch it."

"It is disrespectful," she demurred.

"It is not disrespectful when I invite you to do it. Touch me."

So the woman stretched forth her fingers—but she did not touch him. To her, it seemed, there was nothing there to touch.

"You are a ghost!" she cried.

"To you I am a ghost," he said. "You do not believe and so you cannot touch my flesh. Nor can I touch yours."

"But I am not a ghost," she countered.

He stretched forth his hand to touch hers, but there was no contact.

They looked at one another.

"One of us is not real," the woman said at last. "Which is it?"

"It is you," the Lord replied.

"Can I become real?"

"Yes."

"How?"

"I must reach in and seize the heart of stone that lies within your chest. I will crush it and replace it with another heart. Then your flesh will become real."

"Will it hurt?" she said.

"Yes," said he, "for I will do it all at once. Others have allowed me to do it bit by bit. It doesn't hurt as much, that way."

"And what if I refuse to let you do it?"

"Then you will become the ghost you already are."

The woman considered a moment and then shook her head and said, "I cannot believe in such a fable. You said you could not touch me anyway. My heart is flesh, not stone. Go ahead and try to touch it, and you will see for yourself."

The Lord once more stretched out his hand. It passed right through her chest and she felt it grasp the innermost part of her. The hand began to squeeze. There was a mighty rumble, a creaking and a screeching. The woman could not catch her breath for the pain and thought she would scream aloud.

But just then she looked upon the face of the Lord and saw that he was in pain, too; that, if anything, his pain was twice as great as hers, three times, ten times. She was so transfixed by the sight of his pain that she forgot about her own.

And then it was over. There was a sound and sensation of shattering, then a cold and windy emptiness, and lastly a soft and glowing fire.

She looked down. Her flesh was glowing. She looked at the Lord. He had lowered his hands. She saw, clearly now, the wound in his side.

"May I?" she said.

"Yes," he answered her.

She reached out and touched his wound, and this time she felt it.

"You are real," she said in wonder.

"And therefore," he said, "so are you."

Then he led her in through the gates.

Which?

A MAN ASKED THE apostle at the gate how he might enter.

"Present me with your baptism," she replied, "and I will let you in."

The man paused.

He paused some more.

At last he said, "Which baptism do you want?"

The apostle said, "How many do you have?"

"Three," said the man.

"Let me see them," she replied.

The man took out his three baptisms and laid them before the apostle.

"Tell me about them," she said.

"This is the first," said the man. "It was laid upon me against my will when I was a newborn." He set it off to one side.

Then he held up the next one. "This second," he continued, "I chose for myself, when I came to believe, many years later." He gazed upon it awhile and set it next to the first.

"And finally," he said, pointing to the third, "this one was required of me when I joined a community that would not recognize either the first or the second."

The apostle said, "I can accept only one baptism. Which do you wish to give me?"

The man looked down upon his three baptisms and reflected upon them.

"The third," he said, "belonged to the community, and I wanted it because I wanted them. The second belonged to me and was my own doing. But I did not want the first one at all. Therefore it must be God's. For I could not have wanted the second and the third if I had not already been given the first."

So he picked up the first baptism and presented it to the apostle. She took it and bade him welcome, and he entered in.

Accumulation

"I AM HERE," THE woman announced. "I'm sure you have been expecting me."

"Yes," said the apostle.

"I have brought quite a lot along with me," she continued. She indicated a pile of shiny black boxes tied with even shinier black ribbons on display at her feet. "Here, first, is my tithe. Second, my volunteer hours at the soup kitchen. Third, my many terms on church council. Fourth, countless cleaning and reorganization projects at both the church and various charities. Fifth, nearly two hundred potluck suppers prepared and cleaned up after. Sixth, eighty-two petitions that I sponsored and gathered signatures for. Seventh, more than a hundred thousand dollars raised through sponsored walks. Eighth, multiple overnights at the homeless shelter. Ninth, the suicide hotline. Tenth, altar guild."

The apostle regarded the woman's accumulation of boxes with interest. "Thank you," he said at last.

The woman looked at him expectantly. "Aren't you going to take them?"

"They are not for me," he said. "They have already gone to those who needed them."

"But I have brought them for you. Or rather, for *him*."

"He has no need of them either."

The woman stamped her foot. "Then what good are they?"

"Much good," said the apostle. "As I said, they have already gone to those for whom they were intended."

"Then what I am to do with them?"

"You may leave them there."

"Here? Out here? Don't they come in with me?"

"There is no need of them within."

"Then they were all for nothing!"

"They were not for nothing. They have already gone to those for whom they were intended," said the apostle for the third time.

"But then I must enter empty-handed!" she protested.

"Yes," said the apostle.

"With nothing but myself!"

"Yourself is all that is required."

"It is not enough."

"It is, in fact," observed the apostle, "more than you are willing to give."

"Nonsense," said the woman.

"Then come in," said the apostle.

The woman regarded him with suspicion. Then she clucked and said, "If you won't help me carry them in, I'll just have to do it myself." She tried to pick up all the boxes. But she didn't have hands enough to manage them all at once, and she would not leave any behind, lest they disappear the moment she passed through the gates.

For a long time she struggled to hold them all.

The apostle said again, "There is no need of them here. Come in without them. Come with yourself only."

"They *are* myself," snarled the woman in reply. "And if you don't want them, you don't want me. I will take them to where we both are wanted."

She managed, for a moment, to hold all ten boxes at once and took a few steps away from the gates. Then three of them fell clattering to the ground. For a long time she busied herself arranging them again, and when all were in place, she set off once more.

And so she continued, with slow but steady progress, until the apostle could see her no more.

•   E I G H T   •

Shout

A MAN CAME TEARING up to the pearly gates. He was shouting and continued to shout at the top of his voice.

He shouted of such things that do not happen, and thus are forgotten about, within those gates. He shouted of horrors and terrors, of evil deeds done and endured. He shouted of hatred, grief, and contempt. He shouted of loss, heartbreak, and dissolution. He shouted of a humanity wounded beyond endurance. Indeed, it was on account of these very things that he had arrived at the pearly gates far sooner than the normal time allotted to a human life.

The apostle knew well of such matters but also that he ought not attend to them himself. He summoned the Lord.

The Lord came out of the gate and stood before the man.

The man continued to shout. He repeated all that he had said before.

The Lord listened, very carefully.

The man finished and began again.

The Lord still listened.

It went on like this for a very long time.

At last the man was out of voice and breath, and he stopped.

"I have heard you," said the Lord. "Do you wish to say it again?"

"I cannot stop saying it," whispered the man in his ragged voice. "It erupts out of me. I could not hold it in if I wished. I would be free of it, but it is inscribed upon my very flesh. See here."

He held out his hands and arms and showed the Lord how all the story of the evil he experienced and the evil he returned was written right into his skin, in a dark red ink as if of blood. He pulled up the legs of his trousers and showed the same story written there. It was on his feet, on his back, even on his face; it was written deepest and darkest in his many scars. Every inch of his body was covered with the horrific tale.

The Lord held up his hands. The man saw the holes in them. Without needing to be told what to do, he placed his palms against the Lord's.

At that very moment, the ink on his flesh began to blur and bleed. It ran together; it flowed toward his hands. First his toes were clear, then his knees. His ears and shoulders lost their crimson flush. The whole history of his woe pooled and concentrated in his hands. Then all at once it drained out of them and, so it appeared, into the hands of the Lord.

The man dropped his hands. He looked at himself, clean and clear. Even his scars were healed and gone.

"Amen," he said.

He looked back up at the Lord. The wounds in the Lord's hands were still visible.

"Lord," he said, "I am whole. But you are not."

"So it is," said the Lord. "I am the only one who bears wounds within the city. I bear mine always. But you will never be wounded again. Do you have any more wish to shout?"

"None whatsoever," said the man.

Then the Lord grasped the man's whole and clean hand with his wounded one, and together they passed through the gate.

NINE

Two by Two

TWO WOMEN ARRIVED AT the gate at the same time.

They had never met face to face before, but they knew each other at once. For each had around her neck the insignia of the other's enemy.

The Lord was waiting for them.

One of the women turned to him and said, "Lord, I died for you. My blood was shed on your behalf."

The other said, "As was mine, Lord. I too died for your name's sake."

The first woman said, "But Lord, it was her people who killed me. They claimed to worship your holy name, but they took my life."

The second woman said, "Her people did the same to me. Claiming to be your followers, they killed me, though I too am one of your followers."

"You cannot truly belong to the Lamb, or you would not have slain one of his own," said the first to the second.

"You are the one who is mistaken, for none of his own would put to death another member of his body."

They both turned to the Lord.

"Which of us belongs to you, Lord?" they said together.

He replied, "You both belong to me. You both gave your lives for me. But if you both belong to me, then you belong to each other as well."

The two women regarded each other with surprise.

"A place is prepared for you. You will enter into joy together."

The women looked at their feet.

"Only one matter remains," said the Lord. "It is the insignia around your necks. You must decide together: either both of you will wear your own, or neither of you will wear them at all. This is a matter of freedom: I leave the choice to you."

The two women continued to gaze at their feet. At last the first one raised her head and spoke.

"I could take mine off," she said to the other woman, "and you could take off yours too. And then the point of contention between us would be gone. And yet—"

The second woman continued, as if the thought were her own: "And yet by these insignia we are bound to others, just as we now know we are bound to each other."

"If we are not to break the bond between us, then how shall we break the bond with the others?" said the first.

The second replied, "Therefore we shall both wear the insignia and enter into joy together. And perhaps our reconciliation in heaven will effect a reconciliation on earth."

The first woman said, "Is it good, Lord?"

The Lord said, "It is good."

So with one hand on the insignia, and one hand in the other's, the two martyrs walked into the city together.

Hidden

A MAN STOOD AT the gates, holding a large and weighty sphere in his hands. It was ivory in color and lavishly decorated with the finest tendrils and twists interlocking in a pattern of astonishing intricacy.

The apostle said, "Welcome."

The man looked uncertainly at the apostle, then down at the sphere he held in his hands. "I don't know why I have this," he said hesitatingly.

"It looks to me like faith," the apostle replied.

"I think so, too," said the man, "but I am quite certain it is not *my* faith."

"Why not?" asked the apostle.

The man took a deep breath and said, "It is too big, for one thing." He gazed at it a while longer and then added, "And it is much too beautiful. And complex." He looked up at the apostle. "I think I have it by mistake."

The apostle said, "Do you know whose it is?"

"I believe," said the man, "it is my wife's."

"She is already in here," said the apostle.

"I know. Or at least, I hoped so," said the man.

"Then she left it for you," suggested the apostle, pointing to the sphere, which seemed to glow faintly from within.

"I know she meant it kindly, but what good does that do me? I cannot claim it as my own; I have already confessed to you that it is not. I know better than to expect to be admitted with someone else's faith."

"Hand it to me," said the apostle.

The man placed the sphere in the apostle's hands.

The apostle lifted the sphere up high and then, with all his force, hurled it to the ground.

It shattered into a million pieces.

The man gasped in dismay. "It was so beautiful!" he protested.

But the apostle was already on his knees, rooting among the shards and fragments. All at once he straightened up and cried, "Aha!" in triumph. He held something between his fingers.

"What is it?" said the man.

"Hold out your hand," said the apostle.

The man did, and in it the apostle placed a very tiny sphere, mustard-colored.

"What is it?" said the man.

"It is *your* faith," said the apostle. "Your wife's faith sheltered it and made sure it arrived here intact."

The man gazed at the tiny little thing. "Is it enough?" he asked.

"It is enough," said the apostle.

And the man entered in.

Too Many Gates

A WOMAN FOUND HERSELF at the pearly gates, with hints of the golden city winking from within, shining radiantly without sun or moon. It was exactly as she had hoped.

She approached one of the gates built upon a foundation of jasper and addressed herself to the apostle.

"The jasper is so very beautiful," she said. "It is clearly the ideal foundation for this gate of pearl. Nothing else would do."

"On the contrary," said the apostle, "eleven other precious stones have done just as well. Look, and you will see the others on this side: sapphire and agate. If you were to walk all the way around, you would see also emerald, onyx, and carnelian; chrysolite, beryl, and topaz; chrysoprase, jacinth, and amethyst."

At this, the woman took note of her surroundings for the first time. Indeed, there was not only one pearly gate. There were many pearly gates: twelve, to be precise. Not one of them had a door. All the gates stood open, and through them thousands upon thousands were streaming. She looked back and saw many more eagerly waiting to press through and enter the heavenly city.

"I thought there was but one gate," she said.

"There are twelve," replied the apostle.

"So many," continued the woman, "without doors. Anyone might come in."

"Yes."

"But—but—" stuttered the woman. She stopped, troubled.

"You may come in, too," said the apostle.

"Twelve gates!" repeated the woman. She stepped a few paces back from the jasper foundation and glanced to the side, toward the sapphire and agate gates, where other apostles were welcoming in the masses.

"They are all the same," said the apostle. "It matters not by which one you enter."

"Oh, as to that," said the woman dismissively, "it's not a question of *which* gate is better or worse. Only that there are so many, and always open. It seems so—to be frank—promiscuous."

"Prodigal," suggested the apostle.

"Exactly!" cried the woman. "And prodigal means badly behaved, irresponsible, spendthrift."

"Here it means instead lavish, extravagant, and bounteous."

"I just wouldn't have thought it of heaven." The woman frowned. "No filter, no screen. *Anyone* might come in!"

"When will you?"

The woman shook her head. "I'm just not sure about this," she said. "It wasn't what I was expecting. Maybe I have come to the wrong place."

"This is the place, I assure you."

"I'm afraid I can't take your word for it. I don't know you; how can I trust you? Where are your credentials?"

The apostle laughed. "I can offer nothing that would convince you," he said. "Only the fact that I am here."

"But twelve gates! Standing open at all times! Why, anyone might just march up and claim to be an apostle! And claim that *this* is heaven! I have my doubts. Excuse me, I hope you won't take offense, but I really must examine the other options before I continue any further."

Without another word, the woman turned and walked away, and the apostle quickly lost sight of her.

Do Not Hinder Them

THE LORD NOTICED A gaggle of children outside the gates. They were on their knees, scrabbling in the dirt, gathering something up, putting what they found in their pockets or clutching it tightly in their hands.

"Children," said the Lord, "what are you finding?"

The children turned, rose, and raced over to the Lord. They seized his hands, tugged at his robe, hugged his legs, sat on his feet.

The tallest child spoke for them all. "Look," she said, holding up a handful of her treasures to him, "acorns."

"Heaps of 'em!" cried another, smaller child. "Maybe even... seventy-two!"

"No! More than that! There's at least a hundred an' fifty-*three*!" shouted an even smaller child.

The Lord examined their grubby uplifted hands. "These," he said, "are very special acorns. They never had a chance to grow in the first life. But their time has come. It was very good of you to gather them in."

The children beamed.

"Follow me," he said, and he led them through a gate of pearl into the golden city.

Some way in he stopped at the edge of a pasture, full of grass and flowers but no trees.

"Plant them here," he said.

The children dug into the pliant earth with their thick little fingers, and in each hole they poked an acorn. Lovingly they covered each acorn over with earth, as if tucking a well-loved teddy bear into bed.

"Will you water them?" asked the Lord.

The children rushed off to the river, bright as crystal. They cupped their hands and filled them up and tiptoed back, careful not to lose a single drop, and poured the water over the planted acorns.

"Now we shall see," said the Lord.

The children clustered around him and waited.

In hardly any time at all, a sprout poked out of each little grave. The sprout split at the top into two leaves, then four, then a whole wreath of them. From the midst of each wreath a spray of flowers burst free in dazzling colors; and just as quickly the petals dropped away as the fruit formed in its place. Each fruit grew to ridic-ulous, enormous, impossible size—still upheld by the spindly little sprout—and each was wrapped in a pod that was in turn modestly shielded by a papery husk.

Then all at once, with a sound like bells tinkling, the seedpods cracked and split open. Each child rushed forward and caught in its small arms a baby.

"Look what mine grew!" called one to another. They compared weight and length and hair and noses.

The Lord laid his hands upon each one, and then he charged the children to carry the babies further into the city.

"There are those who have waited long to see their faces," he said.

THIRTEEN

Tiny

"HERE! HERE! I'M DOWN here!" cried the man.

The Lord glanced down and saw the tiny man, arms waving and flailing to catch his attention.

"You are exceptionally small," he observed.

"It's confusing," the man replied. "Most of my life I have been exceptionally large."

"Yes." The Lord waited.

"I have always consumed," the man continued. "Food and drink above all. But other things too. Things to keep and things to throw away. Big and flashy things. Small and subtle things. Cheap things and expensive things."

"Was there ever enough?"

"No, never. The more I had, the more I wanted. The satisfaction of the appetite inflamed it. I didn't know it then. I'm not sure why I know it now."

"Did you consume only things?" said the Lord.

The tiny man dropped his eyes. "No," he confessed. "I consumed people as well."

"That is why there is so little left of you," commented the Lord. "You thought you were consuming things, but they were consuming you. You thought taking the humanity of others would make more of yours, but it only diminished you."

"Then it is a miracle," said the man, "that there is as much of me left as there is."

"You are correct," said the Lord. "It is a miracle."

The tiny man said, "I would like to come in. But I think in there, amidst so many big people, I would be trampled."

"There is a way to grow to your full stature," said the Lord.

"Please show me the way," said the man.

The Lord knelt down. He cupped his hands together. At once they were filled with wine. "Drink of it," he said.

The tiny man scrambled up the Lord's fingers, leaned over the edge of his thumb, and drank.

He began to cough.

Out came the many things he had consumed over the course of his life. He coughed and coughed, ever more violently. A never-ending cascade of stuff tumbled out of his mouth.

With each cough, he grew a little in size.

After some time, the coughing stopped. The tiny man was now a half-sized man. He looked at himself. "I'm afraid I'm not done yet," he said.

The Lord stood up, leaned forward, and held out his open palm. There was a piece of bread in it. "Eat this," he commanded.

The mid-sized man heaved a great sigh, but he ate the bread.

At once his skin erupted in boils. In agony he fell to the ground. The boils were enormous: the length of his forearm, the width of his stomach, the breadth of his thigh. They festered; they popped. From the open wounds people climbed out, people he had consumed. Some were women. Some were men. Some were children. They shook themselves free of his blood and entrails. The Lord laid his hands on them, washed them clean, and guided them in through the open gate.

After all the people had walked free from the boils, the man's skin knit itself back together. When he was whole, he stood up. He was able to look the Lord in the eye. He was full size once more.

"I am so large," he said, "and yet so light."

The Lord said, "You will be larger and lighter when you join the company of your sisters and brothers."

"I would like that," said the man, and he walked through the gate to find them.

I Repent

"I REPENT," SAID THE woman at the gate.

"Of what?" said the Lord.

"When I was a girl, I loved to play sports more than anything else. I spent countless hours practicing and refining my skills."

"That is not a sin. You cannot repent of that," said the Lord.

"Oh," said the woman, confused. "Well, then, I repent of all the questions I asked. I couldn't hold back the doubt when people said things I didn't think were true. I was always asking questions in my mind, even when I didn't say anything out loud."

"That also is not a sin."

"It isn't? Then I need to repent of feeling afraid. I did so often. So many things threatened on all sides."

"And again," said the Lord, "that is not a sin."

"In that case," the woman said, "I had better repent of my desire to work, and work hard. I was never satisfied with the little I had to do and always felt like I was wasting my time, but I suppose I should have valued all the free time I had to do as I pleased."

The Lord shrugged and shook his head.

"For heaven's sake," said the woman. "Then I repent of having liked this music and that artist and those hobbies, for my specific sense of humor and interest in such politics and indifference to particular manners and enjoyment of certain foods."

"I am afraid," said the Lord, "that you have yet to confess a single actual sin."

"But this is ridiculous!" cried the woman. "You don't mean to say that I am sinless?"

"Not at all," the Lord replied. "You are most certainly a sinner. But none of the things you have named are sins."

"But," protested the woman, "I have been told all my life that those were my sins. I have been scolded and shamed for them more times than I can count."

"They were wrong," said the Lord simply.

"Do you mean to say," the woman whispered, "that though my life has been one of endless, dull, afflicting repentance, I have never actually repented at all?"

"If you had repented of real sins," said the Lord, "you would have found relief and rest. That you never found either is the proof that you were misinformed about your sins."

The woman exhaled a heavy sigh.

"I feel much lighter now," she said.

The Lord explained, "That is because the false shame has been lifted off of you."

"Can I go in now?"

"It still remains for you to repent of your true sins."

The woman knit her eyebrows. "I'm not sure," she said haltingly, "that I would even know them if I saw them."

"If you wish, I can show them to you."

"Please do."

The Lord did.

"*Those* are my sins?" the woman shouted in astonishment. "But I never knew!"

"You didn't," agreed the Lord, "but you do now."

"May I take a moment?"

"As long as you need."

The woman observed her sins for some time. They were terrible to face.

At last she said, "Yes, I see now. Those are sins indeed. I wish I had known sooner and not done so much damage. But can I be freed from them, too?"

"You can," said the Lord, "and you are."

And he accompanied her in.

FIFTEEN

Right Answer

"I AM HERE," THE man said. "I do not ask for entry on my own behalf. I have been a sinful man and have no claim to be here on my own merits. I ask for entry only on account of the Lamb of God whose blood has washed away my sins." Then he smiled a great smile, for he knew he had given the right answer.

"For that reason, you may enter," said the sentry at the gate.

The man stepped forward, then hesitated. He looked around him, at the gate to his left and the gate to his right.

"I notice the others," he remarked. "They are pouring in through the doors. Do they say what is required first? Does someone check to hear them speak aright?"

The sentry said, "Those who come in do so on account of the Lamb of God. It is no different from what you said yourself."

"I'm only curious," said the man. "What do they say?"

"What they say," replied the sentry, "is not your concern."

"I only want to know if they say what I said."

"It is not for me to tell you what they say. But they enter for the same reason that you do: the blood of the Lamb."

"But do they *know?* Do they know that is why they may enter?"

"When they enter, they know."

"No, no," said the man. "I mean, did they know *before?*"

"That also is not your concern," said the sentry.

"Which is to say that they are not being admitted according to protocol," the man retorted, drawing himself up tall. "Laxity where one least expects it. I'm afraid I'll need to speak to your superior."

"There is none superior to me."

"Nonsense," said the man. "I'm sure there are many—apostles, prophets, patriarchs. Why, the Lord himself. In fact, this is such a serious matter I cannot settle for anyone less. I demand you bring the Lord to me."

"I am here," said the sentry, for he was himself the Lord.

The man recoiled in shock. "You?" he cried.

"Did you not know me before?" said the Lord.

At those words, the man wept bitterly. "I did not," he said. "But I know you now."

"It is enough," said the Lord. "Come in."

SIXTEEN

Send Me Back

"SEND ME BACK!" SHE wailed. "Send me back!"

"You will not be sent back," said the apostle.

"But I'm not finished!" she shrieked. "There's so much left to be done!"

"There is," agreed the apostle, "but others will take up the mantle. It is your time to rest."

"I don't want rest! I despise rest! I loathe it!" She rent her shirt with her own hands. "They need more help. They can't do it alone!"

"They are not alone."

"They need *me!*"

The apostle's voice became gentle. He rested a hand on her shoulder. "They don't need you," he whispered. "You played your part valiantly and now you are done. They will carry on without you."

A scream escaped from the woman's lips. She shriveled like emptied wineskins and lay limp on the portal.

"There is nothing left to me," she croaked. "I'm gone. Empty. Useless. I have nothing left to give."

"You have given everything," said the apostle. "But you have received nothing. The time is past for giving. To enter here, you must receive."

"I don't want to," she squeaked from her collapsed state. "I won't take from those who need it more than I."

"You need it, and your receiving takes from no one else."

"I don't need it. I have always pulled my own weight."

"And yet now, though you weigh almost nothing, you are too weak to pass through these doors alone."

"I have always been strong," she whispered. "I can't, I won't, I don't—"

"You must," said the apostle.

"Let me at least—"

"Not even that," said the apostle.

"I would not be a beggar," she breathed.

"You spent your life serving beggars, yet you hold them in contempt. Come now, receive as a beggar, and be exalted."

She tried to say something but she was out of voice.

The Lord came forth and laid his hands on her withered body. At once she began to grow again, to fill out, to stretch up tall, to glow.

She looked up at him. "Is it wrong that I no longer wish to go back?"

"The only thing to do now is go forward," he answered her, and so she went forward.

Camel

THE APOSTLE COULD ALREADY see it approaching from a long ways off. What it was, at first, she could not make out. She squinted and stared. Only once it had come quite close could she make sense of its massive size and perplexing shape.

It was a great concatenation of stuff. Every imaginable thing under the sun, bolted, glued, or stuck together. Clothes hangers, clothespins, and clothes to go on them. Cars, crates, and cranes. Appliances and artworks, boats and bathtubs, handkerchiefs and houses, jewels and jets.

Surrounding, enveloping, and trailing after the chain of stuff was packaging, wrappers, acres of tangled tape; and caught inside of that, no end of used-up, worn-down, tossed-out stuff. The whole assemblage was as tall as the heavenly city itself and shook the firmament beneath as it clumped right up to the gates.

The apostle watched with interest as the lump of stuff finally reached her. It was much too large to get in. It had no head, no face, no arms, but evidently it wanted to enter.

Undeterred by the narrow gate, it heaved itself against the wall of the city.

The lump shook; the firmament shook; but the walls of the city remained unmoved.

The lump backed up and flung itself against the gate once more. The tremendous vibration that it sent backward through itself made chunks of the garbage go flying off to the sides. Somewhere in the ether they vanished.

The lump redoubled its efforts and once again assaulted the city.

Still the city stood immovable. The shock detached a number of larger articles at the lump's edges and margins.

This seemed to infuriate the lump. Again it threw itself against the city; again and again and again. The more its own body broke and shattered, the greater violence with which it turned to its attack.

On it went. Other apostles gathered to watch. In another kind of time, aeons might have passed.

Until, at last, there was nothing left to shatter away, and the tiny life inside its massive shell crawled free from the debris all around. It was a person, so thin and slight as to be hardly visible. The person crawled forward to the portal of the gate and kissed the gleaming pearl.

"So long," he gasped, "so long have I carried that weight. And never till now did I find anything hard enough to break me free. Praise and honor and glory to these walls, these immovable walls, these firm foundations, these unrelenting stones! Glory upon them that have set me free!"

"I know what better deserves your praise, and I will show you the way," said the apostle, and she led him into the city.

• E I G H T E E N •

Thief

"Now wait just one minute," said the woman. She was patting her cloak down, hands diving into pockets.

The Lord waited, quietly, passing no comment on the fact that her foot was halfway over the jeweled foundation, her toe just touching down in the holy city.

"Where is it?" She looked up at him with dismayed and clouded eyes.

"What do you seek?" he asked.

"My—" She stopped. Somehow she didn't like to say.

"Ah," he said. He fished into his own pocket and drew something forth.

It was ugly; that was the only thing that could be said with certainty about it. It seemed to be mostly the color of rust, rough-textured and misshapen but with a suggestion that it had once been something whole, lovely, and useful. It would not have been so terrible had it not seemed so mangled from its now unidentifiable original shape.

Yet the woman did not look upon it with disgust. Relief flooded her face. She smiled up at the Lord. "I should have known you'd have it in safekeeping," she breathed, reaching out for it with both hands.

But the Lord dropped it into his pocket again.

"I did take it from you," he agreed, "but not for safekeeping. Rather, to release you from its claim and put the thing to death."

"To death!" shrieked the woman. "But you are the Lord of life! You don't take life, you give it! How could you even think of killing this poor thing!" She reached out again, as though for a wounded animal.

"It is not this thing that needs to live, but you," said the Lord. "And you cannot live as long as it lives with you. It is much heavier than you think."

She saw his hand move toward the pocket again; she perceived the power in that hand, the power to crush the ugly, rusty, mangled mess into oblivion.

"You are a liar," she said, "and a thief."

"One who has lived long with falsehood has a hard time recognizing truth," the Lord said. "But I will admit to being a thief. I have plundered many others before you of their treasured weights and chains. My life is stronger than these things. But yours is not."

"I want it back," she said.

"It has been your sin," said the Lord. "If you take it back, it will become your death. Better to let me keep it."

"But I love it," wept the woman. "I love it. I have loved it so long."

"It has never loved you."

At this the woman's sad face was riven by something like a passing thunderstorm, but as with a storm, it cleared. In the quiet that followed, she murmured, "No. It has never loved me."

"Come in," said the Lord, gesturing through the gate.

"May I," said the woman softly, but with new strength, "may I see you—do what you do to it?"

"You may," he replied, "but it will hurt."

"Not as much as carrying it." The woman turned her palms toward her face. She perceived how they were covered with deep scratches, seething and infected.

The Lord withdrew the thing from his pocket. It seemed to shrink in his hand, yet grew tougher, angrier, as if preparing for a fight.

But the Lord simply closed his fist around it, and it was gone.

"That was so easy!" exclaimed the woman, delighted.

"Only," said the Lord, "because you had stopped loving it."

"But I would not have stopped loving it," she countered, "if you had not first stolen it from me."

"Come in now," said the Lord.

The Least of These

THE MAN STRODE UP to the gate. "Here I am," he said. "Let me in."

A sentry whose face was veiled stood at the gate and said, "It is customary, first, to meet with the Lord."

"I'm ready," said the man. "Why not? I'm curious to see him after all this waiting."

"As am I to see you," said the Lord. He unveiled his face.

But the man did not see the face he was expecting, the face of the Lord. Instead he saw the face of a beggar who had asked him for food. The man had given him nothing but a kick.

"You!" he shrieked in alarm. "*You* are the Lord?"

In that moment the face changed. It was no longer that of a beggar. Now it was of a child from the country-side who had been hoarding a small glass of water. The man had seized it from the child's hands and drunk it himself.

Before the man could say anything more, the face changed again.

Now it was of a foreigner who had asked for help while lost and alone in the man's country. The man had scoffed and turned aside.

A moment later it was a woman whom he had found naked and vulnerable and so had violated her.

Next, the sick and dying mother he had refused to visit.

Then, in a flickering stream, the thousands of faces of people he had helped to imprison in his service to a wicked power, faces he had never bothered to see in person, faces that in his reckoning belonged to names and numbers but not to bodies, not to families, not to friends, not to the Lord.

"Look what you have done to me," said the Lord.

But the man would not look. He turned and ran in the only direction he could.

Vision

"I THOUGHT," SAID SHE, in a murmur to herself, "that when I arrived here I would behold the Lord himself in all his glory...?"

"Yes," said the Lord.

"Who said that?"

"I did."

"Stop playing tricks on me. Where is the Lord? I want to see him, as promised."

"The one to whom you speak is he."

The woman twisted this way and that. "I don't see anyone." She tilted her head up and down. "I see the walls of the city, and the gates with their pearlescent sheen. But I don't see the Lord—or you either, for that matter. Where are you?"

"I am right in front of you," said he.

"That's ridiculous. If you were in front of me, I'd see you."

"Something obstructs your vision."

The woman began to contradict him, but as she spoke her hand went to her face and she discovered, to her great surprise, a pair of spectacles sitting on her nose.

"How did those get there?" she demanded.

"You have worn them a long time," said the Lord.

"I never knew," she said. "Are they to improve my vision?"

"Quite the contrary," said the Lord. "The lenses are so dark that you can see nothing; not me, nor anyone else. Nor have you ever."

"What a thing to say," retorted the woman. "Of course I've seen you, to say nothing of my husband, and children, and neighbors, and friends!"

"You've worn the glasses so long," said the Lord, "that you no longer even know what vision is."

"Well, you're the Lord, aren't you? Or so you say. Supposedly you can restore sight to the blind. Am I to be an exception to the rule?"

"Do you want your vision restored?"

"Well, of course I do; if it's really gone, that is. Which I doubt," added the woman, with a quiet snicker.

The Lord reached forward and grasped the opaque-lensed frames on either side. He slid them off the woman's face and they ceased to exist.

In the same instant the woman found herself in agony. "My eyes!" she screamed. Light streamed into them as never before, searing her with pain. She shoved the heels of her hands into her eye sockets, trying to block it out. "Give them back to me! This is unendurable!"

But the Lord handed her something else. It was like the branch of a tree, with baubles hanging from the end of each twig. To grasp it she had to peel one hand away from an eye. From the one squinting eye she peeped cautiously.

"What's this?" she said, but upon closer examination she answered her own question. In one bauble she saw her son; in another, her elder daughter, and in yet another, her younger daughter. Grandparents, colleagues, and cousins all came into view.

She stared a long time, fascinated.

"I know them," she said tremulously. "I mean to say, I recognized all of them at once. But they are—so different. I have never seen them clearly before."

The Lord nodded his agreement.

"And if I have not seen *them* clearly," she ventured, "that must mean I also have not seen—?"

At this, the Lord handed her a mirror.

She took the other hand from her other eye and with great effort opened it. Open eyes were still painful. But she lifted the mirror to her face.

An unspeakable sorrow crisscrossed her face.

"This is *me?*" she whispered.

"It is who you have been," said the Lord.

"I am not fit to go in there. I'm not worthy of the company of these dear people. I don't deserve it," she pronounced with desperate finality.

"It's true; you do not," said the Lord.

Then he took her hand and led her into the city.

First Is Last

"I'm tired of waiting," said the man to nobody in particular, despite the fact that many people stood around him, both in front and in back.

"I never had to wait before," he said even louder.

"I am not the sort of person who waits," he announced.

With that he pushed his way past the people in front of him, who seemed to melt away at his ungentle touch. He counted down the people ahead of him and deftly slipped in front of them, from the twenty-fourth to the twelfth to the sixth to the third to the second to the first.

But as he stepped in front of the first person, he discovered, to his great dismay, that he was not the first. He was at the back of a longer line than ever; at least fifty people were waiting ahead of him.

He peered off to the side and saw another line there. It looked shorter. He glanced around and darted over.

But when he got there the line was longer than where he'd been before. And he was again at the back of it.

"Ah, I get it," he said, laying a finger to his temple. "It's an optical illusion. A trick. Go to the beginning and find yourself at the end. But go to the end and find yourself at the beginning!"

Pleased at his own cleverness, the man ran back to the first line and stationed himself at the back. "Here I am!" he cried to no one in particular. "I'm at the end. So now—"

He waited. Briefly.

He was still at the end.

"Now this really is not fair," he complained. He tapped the shoulder of the person ahead of him. "Don't you think this is unfair?"

"Yes," said the one in front of him. "But fairness has nothing to do with it."

"Exactly as I suspected," pronounced the man with satisfaction. "I'm disappointed in this place. Really I am. I had expected better. I thought unfairness would come to an end here."

"Oh no," said the one in front. "Unfairness only continues. But it is a different order of unfairness."

"Eh?" said the man. "How's that?"

"In the previous life you knew unfairness. You were born to wealth. You were awash in attention. You never hungered. You knew no thirst. You got what you liked. You gave when you wished. You worked as you pleased."

"I'm not entirely sure I would call that unfair—" the man began in protest.

"And these ahead of you, they felt the unfairness more keenly than you did, for they waited, and hungered, and thirsted, and struggled, and none of them gained what they sought."

"But that wasn't my doing!" objected the man. "I didn't choose that life for them any more than I chose mine for myself!"

"Precisely. It was unfair. And here also it is unfair. They will enter into joy before you."

Then the speaker was gone.

The man realized who it had been.

And he wondered whether he should stay on at the end of the line, or look for another place where things weren't quite so unfair.

TWENTY-TWO

Gray

THE APOSTLE FOUND THE woman crumpled to one side of the gate, cradling something in her arms.

"What is it?" he asked gently.

"It's what I brought with me," she wept.

"Can I see it?"

She held it up to him. He saw a bundle of gray and ragged cloth. He gently pushed one fold of the cloth away. Inside was a gray mass, formless. It reflected no light.

"Won't you come in?" said the apostle.

"With this only?" the woman protested. "I've been watching the others who come here. One carried a fractal filigree with an iridescent sheen. Another had a bouquet of lilies of a thousand subtle fragrances. Still another, plumage in azure and cream and glittering obsidian. What extravagance! But all I have is this nothingness. I'd be ashamed to walk in there with it."

"You did not watch carefully enough," said the apostle. "Look again."

Just then another woman approached the gate. Her hands were full to overflowing with the richest deep-green foliage, tendrils bouncing gleefully, shoots sprouting every which way. She smiled broadly as she looked at the apostle.

"Here it is!" she cried, holding out the luscious plant.

"Thank you," said the apostle gravely as he took it from her. "Well done, good and faithful servant."

"It was my joy and honor," replied the woman, but her fingers flexed, as if uncomfortable without a firm grip on the plant.

The apostle admired the greenery in his hands. Then he drew his palms closer together. As he did so, the plant shrank in size. It got smaller and smaller as the hands came closer and closer until, at last, the palms met in the position of prayer. When they touched, the plant winked out of existence.

"What have you done?" shrieked she who brought it.

"It has served its purpose," explained the apostle. "And served it well. But in here, it is of no further use to you; indeed, in there, it would damage both you and others."

"But it was a good thing! A beautiful thing!"

"I agree. But its time is over."

"Who will ever see it now?"

"The Lord has seen it, and it pleased him while it lived. Now it pleases him to see you only."

The woman's face turned ashen. "I don't know that I want to go in there anymore," she whispered.

But at this, the woman with the gray bundle found her feet. She shoved her uncomely package into the apostle's hands. "Do the same with mine," she cried.

He did. The gray monstrosity also winked out of existence.

She smiled hugely, gathering up the other woman in her smile.

But that one pled to the apostle, "Is there no difference between us at all then?" She gestured with an embarrassed finger to the first woman.

"Of course there is," he replied. "Yet all have this in common: whoever enters here enters empty-handed."

"That is a joy for *her*," complained the woman formerly of the plant.

"And it is a sorrow for *you*," said the woman formerly of the gray bundle. "As it turns out, I know a great deal about sorrow. Maybe, if you let me, I can show you the way in."

She held out a hand.

The other woman looked at it for some time. Then she took it.

They walked in through the gate together.

Grace

"At last," he said. "Peace. Harmony. Acceptance. I hoped for so long, and here it is at last." He stood back, admiring the translucent jasper-colored walls, the shining pearl portals, the shimmering river glimpsed through the doorway.

He approached the door and stopped short.

"I don't understand," he said.

"Come in," said the Lord.

"But—how can I?" puzzled the man. "You are blocking my way, I think." He couldn't quite make out what he was seeing.

"I am not blocking your way," said the Lord. "I *am* the way."

The man shook his head. "I don't understand."

"Come to me, walk through me, and you will enter in."

The man's brows knit together. "That's a funny kind of welcome," he said. "I still say you're blocking the way." To himself he said, I will simply walk to the next gate. There are so many of them; surely there will be an easier way in.

But at the next gate he again found the Lord, filling the whole doorway as if stretched out and pegged to either side.

"I don't think you really *want* people to come in," he protested. "A welcome is an open door, with no impediments."

"This is an open door," said the Lord. "Nothing will prevent you from walking through and into the city."

"You lay a pretty strong claim to this place," grumbled the man.

"It is mine," said the Lord. "Though I gladly share it with all who would enter."

"But you make no mistake about your ownership."

"No," agreed the Lord, "that I do not."

"Seems pretty ungracious to me. I wouldn't do it that way."

The Lord again agreed with the man. "Perhaps," he added, "you would like to explore the alternatives."

"Yes, I would!" exclaimed the man. "Point the way."

The Lord nodded in the opposite direction. "Over there," he said, "you will find other doorways. It is equally easy to walk through them; no one will stop you."

"As it should be," declared the man. He walked off.

• TWENTY-FOUR •

Telling

WHEN SHE OPENED HER mouth to speak, no words came out.

Instead, a little puff of smoke.

She knit her brow and tried again.

This time, a shower of dust.

Then a foggy mist.

Then a scattering of dried grass.

Then a cascade of ashes.

In rage and frustration she sucked in a deep breath and expelled it with all her might. A tornado popped out and deflated at once.

She waved her hands at the apostle, jumped up and down, stomped her foot.

The apostle, knowing when matters were beyond his ken, sent a summoning word into the city. In short order a seraph emerged, holding a pair of tongs.

In the grip of the tongs was a fiery coal.

Before the woman knew what was happening, the coal was laid against her lips, searing them.

Her first sound was a shriek but it stopped abruptly, for as soon as the coal burned, it also cauterized and healed the wound.

She gathered her breath for outrage but the words she spoke were: "I NEVER TOLD THE TRUTH!"

The words did a strange thing: they took visible form. They hung in the air. They were solid, multidimensional, like granite streaking through space and time. They looked like they could knock her over.

Somehow she knew she had to deal with them, or they would deal with her.

She reached for the I. It came to her hands. She pressed it into her chest. It sank in deep and stayed there.

She thought about what to do with the NEVER. It seemed heavier than the other words. She wanted to rid herself of it, but it bobbed in the air and loomed ever closer.

At last she grabbed it. She held it tight and began to scrub her body with it. Off sloughed colorless curls and shreds. She scrubbed and scrubbed, and from beneath the thick encrusting, her own skin gleamed through. The more she scrubbed, the smaller the NEVER got, like a bar of soap. When she was thoroughly polished, the last fragment of NEVER dissolved and disappeared.

She looked down admiringly at her shiny limbs. She'd never imagined how good it would feel to be free of the layers and layers covering her.

In strength now, she reached for the TOLD. She wrapped it into a cone so it formed a megaphone. Holding it in one hand, she reached with the other hand for the connected pair of THE TRUTH. It had looked to her as heavy as the other words, but when she grasped it found it to be surprisingly light, so light that it started to lift her off the ground. She placed it inside the megaphone and turned the narrow end to her lips.

A moment later the walls of the city were echoing back THE TRUTH, as she announced and released what had long been suffocated and disguised. It was like music, intricate counterpoint, scintillating harmonies, under a melody that expanded the hearts of all who heard it.

It took quite a while to finish; there was much to be TOLD.

When the telling of THE TRUTH was complete, the megaphone and its contents drifted out of her hands and into the city.

"Would you like to follow them?" said the apostle.

The woman answered, "Yes," and she did.

• T W E N T Y - F I V E •

Oh No

"Oh, no," said the man. "Oh, no. Oh, *no*."

The Lord regarded him.

"It's not *you*. It can't be *you*. God help me. Are you really who I think you are?"

"I am."

The man stumbled backward as if he had been struck. When he picked himself up, he said, "My entire life has been built on rejecting you."

"You have not only rejected me; you have maligned my name."

"And those who praised it," the man added. He shuddered and pressed on, as if unable to hold it in, "And I have vilified your house. And I have despised your works. And I have mocked your ways. I have been the very embodiment of contempt of you. I have been contempt from head to toe."

The Lord nodded in agreement.

"So now what?" said the man.

"If you have any contempt left to express," said the Lord, "now is a fine time to let it out."

"You want to hear more?"

"There is no reason to leave anything unsaid."

Suddenly the man burst out, "Why did you never *hear* me? Or all the others who cried to you and to the one who claimed to approve of you? Why did you bring us no relief? Why did you show us no mercy? How could you just stand there and look on, all this time, while we, while we..."

All at once the man was upon the Lord. He spat in his face and tore at his hair. He kicked, he punched, he scratched, he bit.

"You fool! You madman! You deluded charlatan! You prayed and hoped like the rest of us and look where it got you!"

"This is where it got me," said the Lord, gesturing to the city through the gate.

But the man didn't hear him. His attack was so frenzied that he plunged, face and hands first, right into the Lord's chest. He tore through the ribcage and dove out the other side, where he collapsed on the ground.

Sprawled out, he looked up at the Lord, who remained whole and intact after the man's boring through the middle of him. But older wounds remained visible elsewhere on his body.

The man looked down at himself. He was covered with blood head to toe, drenched as though he'd been dipped in a well of it.

Then he looked around him and realized that he was within the holy city.

"Why did you let me in?" he asked.

"All who enter here enter by my blood," said the Lord.

"But I assaulted you."

"Though you would not be covered by my blood on account of love, still you found your way to it and through it. It is enough."

The man stood. "Do you love all those who hate you?"

"Them most of all."

"Then I should find more of my kind here."

"You will."

And the man walked on into the heart of the city.

Crowd

T HE APOSTLE WAS SURPRISED to see a thousand enter
all at once, in a rush.

"Will you not speak to each directly and personally?"
he asked the Lord.

"There is time for that," the Lord responded. "First
they need healing and rest."

"I saw the wounds," the apostle acknowledged.
"Grievous. And yet—"

The Lord waited for him to say more.

"You seem quite certain that all of them suffered
for you," said the apostle. "But I suspect not all of them
knew what they were about. Some were much too
young to know you."

"But I knew them," said the Lord. "My name was already upon them."

"Well then," said the apostle, "others were mistaken
for your followers and unlucky."

"Yet they died on account of my name," said the
Lord. "These, too, I welcome in."

The apostle pressed on, "I can grant your reasoning in those cases. But there are others, I fear, who lost faith in you at the end. Their courage dissolved in the face of death. Some of them," the apostle dropped his voice to a whisper, "some of them even cried out that you had forsaken them. Could you vindicate such as these?"

"Dear friend," said the Lord, "when they said that, they were quoting me."

The apostle dropped his eyes to the ground.

"And my Father vindicated me who had said this," the Lord continued. "Will I not then vindicate those who cry out my very words?"

"It is good, Lord," said the apostle.

Himself

"I suppose," said the man, "you expect me to worship you."

"It is the customary preamble to entry," conceded the Lord.

"Ha!" said the man. "I'd rather go to hell, and I know whereof I speak. I saw it on the way here. *I* worship no one."

"They disagree with you," remarked the Lord, gesturing behind the man.

The latter turned and saw great figures, the size of pillars or obelisks, gliding in his direction, faster than their bulk ought to allow.

"Are you threatening me?" demanded the man. "Are these your bouncers? Come to kick me out for not sniveling and groveling like the rest of them?"

"Not at all," said the Lord. "I merely offer you the chance to be united with the lords you have worshiped until now."

They drew closer.

The man began to recognize them, one by one.

First came the Nation, an impressive edifice of brick, but with each thundering step its facade revealed itself with a crack that shed debris in every direction and exposed black holes in its wake.

Then there was History: a jumbled, confusing, unpleasing pattern of disruptive colors and corkscrew threads spiraling off in every direction.

Then Power, an expression of relentless hunger stretched across what passed for its face.

Next came Progress, a drill and a whirligig in one, carving out pits in the ground and attempting to snare the other lords in them with a gleeful, high-pitched whine.

Last of all Humanity. The man could barely bring himself to look at it. It was bruised, bloodied, and bristling with a hatred that seemed to reverberate right to the walls of the city.

They formed a circle around him and closed in.

"It's not fair!" shrieked the man. "You're coercing me! You're trying to terrorize me with these dogs of yours!"

"I have nothing to do with them; you are the one who summoned them," said the Lord. "Send them away and they will obey."

"These monsters, obey me?!" he cried. He was on his hands and knees, shaking.

"The only power they have is your worship."

Power bore down on the man, its vast mouth opening to engulf him.

"Go!" the man whimpered. "Go away! Leave me! I want nothing more to do with you!"

Power withered like a balloon whose air had been let out and blew out of sight with a faint pop.

The man could hardly believe his eyes. He glanced up at the Nation and saw a hole the shape of himself among its bricks. He knew he would be fitted into it and vanish if he delayed a moment longer. "Go! Scram! Leave me alone!" he shouted, and the Nation collapsed into a cloud of dust.

Emboldened by his successes, the man dismissed History, Progress, and Humanity, each of which was reduced to nothing by the man's rebuke.

"Whew," he said, sitting up. "What a relief." Then he chuckled. "That wasn't so hard, once I knew what to say. I didn't need you at all! Nice try, but it backfired on you."

The Lord said nothing.

Then the man heard footsteps. He recognized them instantly.

They were his own.

He forced himself to turn and face the last lord. It was Himself, of colossal size and strength. The Himself was more beautiful than the man really was, more muscular than he really was, more radiant than he really was. There was nothing shabby or shoddy about him at all. If anything, he looked far more godly than the one standing at the gate.

This latter one said, in a calm tone, to the Himself, "You know that you cannot enter here."

The gigantic Himself shrugged, undismayed by the news. But it turned to the smaller version of which it was a replica with a look of pure greed.

"The hour has come at last," it rasped, "to eat you and be done with you. You pathetic, paltry, poor excuse for a person. How I have longed to erase every last trace of you from existence and memory. Now, now, now is my time." Its salivating mouth stretched wide and eager.

The man fell flat on his face. From his muffled mouth came the impassioned plea: "Help me! Save me! Save me from Myself!"

The Lord reached down and plucked up the man between his fingers. In those fingers he shrank, protesting as he shrank, imagining himself to be rendered all the more helpless in the presence of his foe.

But the Lord tucked the tiny man into his side, into a kind of crevice or cave that sheltered him all around.

Then the Himself attacked, flinging its bulk onto the Lord.

The Lord did not flinch or budge.

The Himself shipwrecked on the Lord and burst into a million useless fragments.

Then the Lord stepped through the gate, retrieved the tiny man, and set him down. Once his feet touched the ground, he grew back rapidly to his original size.

"My Lord and my God," he gasped.

Ledger

"It was such a waste," the man complained to the apostle.

"Why do you say that?" she inquired.

"Look here, I have the ledger," said the man. He shifted an enormous leather-bound book from one hand to the other. "I found my name in this column, and don't get me wrong, I'm glad to be here at all! But now look at *this* column next to it."

The apostle leaned in for a closer look.

"This is the column listing all the people whose lives I made a difference to. Whose *eternal* lives I made a difference to, I should clarify." He shook his head. "Now you must know perfectly well how much effort I invested my whole life long in making a difference. I worked really, really hard. I know I'm not the most talented person out there, or the most brilliant, but God knows I tried. I believed it would count for something. And look at the result!"

The apostle smiled warmly. "Look, there is a name written in the adjoining column," she said. "Praise to the Lamb who was slain! All who shelter under the altar rejoice."

"No, no, no, you're seeing it wrong!" exclaimed the man. He had to shift the ledger back to the other hand again because it was so heavy. "There's only *one* name. One name *only!*"

The apostle looked as bewildered as it is possible for an apostle to look.

"Now look at *this* entry," persisted the man. He pointed to the opposite page and a different name. "Just see how many are in the column next to *his* name! Hundreds. Maybe thousands—too many to count."

The apostle began, "Praise to the Lamb," but the man cut her off.

"Compare my life to his," he continued. "Mine was practically worthless. His was a roaring success. Doesn't the unfairness bother you?"

The apostle said, "No one enters on account of success. You need not fear that you will be denied. Indeed, you are warmly anticipated."

"I'm not worried about getting *in*," shouted the man. "My point is that my life was a complete and utter waste of time. *One* person! That all my years and struggles and agonies should add up to just *one!* Whereas he—"

This time the apostle interrupted the man. "I understand you now," she said. "It is so long since I abandoned the world's way of reckoning that it has taken me a while to remember. You still operate according to the principle that *more is better*."

"Is it not?" cried the man.

"More is not better. More is simply more. And here, all more can mean is one, plus another one, plus another one, and so on. It is always the one that takes precedence."

"But is the salvation of a thousand not greatly to be preferred over the salvation of merely one?"

"Not if you are that one person," said the apostle gravely.

"And who is that one person?" scoffed the man. "To tell you the truth, I don't even recognize the name."

"It was never necessary, then," said the apostle.

"So this is all I get!"

"What you get is what everyone gets who enters here. And, through you, this person also gets the same. For which the saints rejoice. The economy here is not the world's economy, you know."

"I suppose this other fellow and I will be greeted as equals, then, imputing to me equal credit I do not deserve."

The apostle's face sobered at this remark. "In truth," she said, "he is not here."

"He's still alive?"

"No. He would not enter."

"Why ever not?" said the man in alarm.

The apostle said softly, "He saw your name, and asked what more he would get than you. When he learned that you were to share equally in the life to come, he became enraged and went away."

This rendered the man silent for some time.

At last he said, "And yet, those thousands—are they still admitted? Even when he has wandered away?"

"Yes, for the means by which they came to know the Lamb is of no consequence," she said.

"Then I am of no consequence," said the man. Before the apostle could dispute his saying, he continued, "And thanks be to God for that! I can enter as a child with empty hands. I am ready for rest."

"It is yours for the taking," said the apostle, and the man walked in.

Another Name

"I CAN'T GO IN there with this name still hanging around me," said the woman.

The Lord saw the name on her back. It was so heavy that it doubled her over.

"I've tried and I've tried but I can't ever seem to get it off my back," she said.

"One of those names was a good name once," observed the Lord.

"I know, and there was a time when I loved to hear it," she agreed. "But it's been chained so long to the other name I can't hear the one without the other anymore. It's been ruined and despoiled. Can't you set me free of it?"

"I can unchain your good name," said the Lord, "and cleanse it for you. Would you like that?"

The woman thought about it, still bent double. At last she said, "Is it wrong to leave an old name behind when a new life begins?"

"Not at all," said he.

"Then, if it's all the same to you, I'd like a completely new name," she said. "If you can get rid of the old one for me."

"I can," he said.

He stepped toward the woman and took the two names in his hands. He snapped the chain that bound them. The bad name he flung down, and it passed through the ground beneath them forever out of sight. The good name he stroked with his hand, as if gently closing its eyelids. Just as gently, it faded, faded, faded till nothing more of it was to be seen.

The woman stood up straight. "That feels wonderful," she said. "The only thing that could make it better would be having a new name of my very own."

The Lord held forth his hand. In it lay a white stone. The woman took it. She looked at it closely. Her face lit up.

"I love it," she said. "Thank you." Then: "Would it be all right if I kept it to myself for a while?"

"You may," said the Lord. "But I don't think you'll want to for long, once you are inside the city. In any case, this is a name that will never tarnish."

"Thank you," she said again.

The Other Place

WHEN SHE ARRIVED AT the pearly gates she was surprised not to find there someone she loved. She did not wish to enter without him, so she left in search of him.

It didn't take long to find him. He wasn't far from the pearly gates at all. But the place he was in was unlike the pearly gates. They shone, but this place seemed to suck all the light from the air. A lovely gentle fragrance floated from the pearly gates; this place reeked of rot and ruin. The pearly gates made the heart sing; this place made the heart curse.

But there was one thing both places had in common: their gates stood wide open.

The pearly gates didn't seem even to have doors, just archways laid open to whomever might wish to enter. But this other place, certainly it had once had gates that closed and locked. Only they didn't anymore. The gates had been wrenched clean off their hinges. The locks and bolts were shattered and scattered across the ground. Cobwebs grew over them as if they hadn't moved in ages. It was as easy to get through to the other place as through the pearly gates and, it would seem, far easier to get out.

Which made it all the more perplexing that the other place was so crowded.

Many people were just outside the gates, crouching or hunched over, leaning up against the twisted wreckage of the doors or lying stretched out on the ground, their hands caressing the broken locks. Others gathered up the fragments and knocked them one against the other. Past them, and beyond the ruined gates, she could see bodies, a great press of bodies, struggling and squeezing and pushing and sometimes outright fighting. It wasn't clear if they were trying to get out or trying to get farther in. Their every effort seemed pointless and futile.

The woman saw the one she was looking for, far at the back of the crowd, but she was too scared to go in. In dismay she retraced her steps the short distance back to the pearly gates.

When she arrived she marched right up to one of the twelve open archways and asked to speak to the Lord. The Lord promptly appeared.

"I can't believe it," the woman said to him. "Look at all of those poor souls, just steps away from your front door, and you leave them there! How could you? I thought your will was to save! How dare you enjoy your peace and light up here and leave them all alone?"

"But I have not left them alone," said the Lord. "I am there. Every day, every hour, every minute."

"To laugh at them? To rejoice in their grief?" said the woman bitterly.

"No," said the Lord, "to invite them to leave. Did you not see the shattered gates?"

"Yes. It looks like a mob rose up in revolt and tore them down."

"It wasn't they who did it," said the Lord. "It was I."

"*You* tore down those gates?" said the woman in wonder.

"And they have never forgiven me for it."

"Why?"

"Because they wish to stay where I am not. And now the gates cannot keep me out."

The woman said, "So the people at the gate of the other place—they are trying to rebuild it?"

"Yes."

"To keep you out?"

"Yes."

"And my—my—" She broke into deep wracked sobbing.

"Yes," said the Lord, with gentleness.

"Promise me you won't leave him," she wept as she passed through the pearly gates. "Promise me you will keep trying."

The Lord turned toward the other place. "I will never leave him," he said. "I will never stop trying."

Sarah Hinlicky Wilson
is the Founder of Thornbush Press.
She serves as Associate Pastor at
Tokyo Lutheran Church in Japan,
where she lives with her husband and son.
She co-hosts the podcast
"Queen of the Sciences:
Conversations between a Theologian
and Her Dad" with Paul R. Hinlicky.
Sign up for her quarterly e-newsletter
"Theology & a Recipe"
and learn more about her other books at:

www.sarahhinlickywilson.com

and

www.thornbushpress.com

by the same author

The Sermon on the Mount: A Poetic Paraphrase

A Guide to Pentecostal Movements for Lutherans

Woman, Women, and the Priesthood
in the Trinitarian Theology of Elisabeth Behr-Sigel